★ **BOOK 5** ★
in the **Classroom 13 Series**

and Heinous

THE HAPPY HALLOWEEN OF
CLASSROOM 13

By **Honest Lee** & **Matthew J. Gilbert**
Art by **Joelle Dreidemy**

LITTLE, BROWN AND COMPANY
New York • Boston

Copyright © 2018 by Hachette Book Group
CLASSROOM 13 is a trademark of Hachette Book Group, Inc.
Cover and interior art by Joelle Dreidemy. Cover design by Véronique L. Sweet.
Cover copyright © 2018 by Hachette Book Group, Inc.

Little, Brown and Company
Hachette Book Group
1290 Avenue of the Americas, New York, NY 10104
Visit us at LBYR.com

First Edition: July 2018

Little, Brown and Company is a division of Hachette Book Group, Inc.
The Little, Brown name and logo are trademarks of Hachette Book Group, Inc.

The publisher is not responsible for websites (or their content) that are not owned by the publisher.

Library of Congress Cataloging-in-Publication Data

Names: Lee, Honest, author. | Gilbert, Matthew J., author.
| Dreidemy, Joelle, illustrator.

Title: The happy and heinous Halloween of Classroom 13 /
by Honest Lee & Matthew J. Gilbert ; art by Joelle Dreidemy.

Description: First edition. | New York : Little, Brown and Company, 2018. |
Series: Classroom 13 ; book 5 | Summary: Tired of being left out of everything,
Classroom 13 itself puts out a bowl of cursed candy on Halloween that changes
everyone into the costume he or she is wearing.

Identifiers: LCCN 2017027419| ISBN 9780316501149 (hardcover) |
ISBN 9780316501156 (trade pbk.) | ISBN 9780316501132 (ebook) |
ISBN 9780316501163 (library ebook edition)

Subjects: | CYAC: Schools—Fiction. | Vengeance—Fiction. | Magic—Fiction. |
Costume—Fiction. | Halloween—Fiction. | Humorous stories.

Classification: LCC PZ7.1.L415 Hap 2018 | DDC [Fic]—dc23

LC record available at https://lccn.loc.gov/2017027419

Printed in the United States of America

LSC-C

Hardcover: 10 9 8 7 6 5 4 3 2 1
Paperback: 10 9 8 7 6 5 4 3 2 1

CONTENTS

CHAPTER 1
Classroom 13's Revenge

The 13th Classroom was not evil—it just didn't like being left out of all the fun.

And the students of Classroom 13 were *always* having fun. Once, they won the lottery and didn't give Classroom 13 any of their money. Another time, they found a magic ~~genie~~ djinn lamp and didn't give Classroom 13 a wish. This other time, they all became super famous and the agent didn't even notice Classroom 13 (...though it certainly showed her). Last month, everyone in Classroom 13 got superpowers—that is, everyone except Classroom 13. (Oh, and Jacob.)

The 13th Classroom was sick and tired of not being included. Now it wanted *revenge*! And for Halloween, it had just the revenge in mind....

It left out a bowl of candy.

You might think that this was nice, but it was *not*. It was a nasty thing to do.

What's that? You don't believe me? You think candy on Halloween is nice? Just wait and see. Sometimes the best *treats* turn out to be *tricks*.

CHAPTER 2
Little Linda
Riding Hood

When schoolteacher Ms. Linda LaCrosse woke up on the morning of Halloween, she was absolutely ecstatic. (That's another word for super-duper happy.)

Halloween was one of her favorite holidays. She had been putting together her costume for weeks. First she got a picnic basket with a little plaid cloth inside. Then she got a little stuffed animal of a wolf. Finally, she got a red cloak. She was going to be Little Red Riding Hood.

For breakfast, she poached her bread in a pot of water and cooked her eggs in the toaster. Her toast was very soggy and her eggs were very dry.

It didn't matter, though, she thought to herself. It was Halloween. She could eat candy instead of a good breakfast. (Which, if you ask me, is a foolish thing to think. Breakfast is the most important meal of the day, and no amount of candy can replace it. Me? I eat cake for breakfast every morning. Cake is a very sensible breakfast.)

After she put on her costume, Ms. Linda looked in the mirror. "Now, Little Red Riding Hood," she said to herself, "I want you to go straight to Grandmother's house. Don't talk to any strangers in the forest. And watch out for wolves!"

Ms. Linda giggled. She skipped merrily all the way to school. When she arrived, she turned on the lights and dusted the shelves. She readied her books and hung the decorations. Finally, she noticed a strange bowl of candy in the center of the room.

"I wonder who put that there," Ms. Linda said. "Probably one of my students. What a thoughtful thing to do. I should take a piece. It would be rude *not* to have at least one."

Ms. Linda picked a piece of candy and tossed it into her mouth. It tasted like chocolate, Worcestershire sauce, and fresh-cut grass.

A moment later, Ms. Linda became very confused. Looking around the room, she asked herself, "Where am I? Where are the woods? And which is the way to Grandmama's house?"

As some of the students walked into the classroom, they waved to their teacher. "Happy Halloween, Ms. Linda," said Dev.

"Halloween? What's Halloween? And who is Ms. Linda?" said Ms. Linda. "My name is Little Red Riding Hood."

"It is?" Mason asked.

"No, it's not," Olivia said sternly. "Your name is Ms. Linda. You're our teacher."

"A teacher?" said Ms. Linda. "Oh, I think not. I don't even go to school. I spend each day going back and forth to Grandmama's house. I deliver her bread and fruit. You see, she's very sick and too weak to travel herself."

"Wow, our teacher is *really* in character," said Liam.

"Who are all of you children? And why are you dressed so strangely?" Ms. Linda asked, hiding behind her desk. The students' costumes terrified her. There was a ghost and a pirate and some kind of zombie. "Never mind who—or *what*—you are. If one of you would be oh so kind enough to point me in the right direction of the woods, I'll be on my way."

"Okay, this is super weird," said Mark, "even for our class."

Ms. Linda—still confused—really *did* think she was Little Red Riding Hood. She pulled the cloak over her head and hid under her desk from the children in their strange outfits.

Everyone was distracted by the odd start to their day, so they didn't hear the 13th Classroom laughing at them. Its revenge had begun.

CHAPTER 3
The Hot Dog

Hugo Houde aimait les hot-dogs. Donc, pour Halloween, il décida de se déguiser en hot-dog. Quand il entra dans la classe, il prit un bonbon dans le bol, le mangea, et s'assit.

Quelques secondes plus tard, Hugo était transformé en véritable hot-dog.

CHAPTER 4
The Two-Headed Horse

Mason scratched his head as twins Mya & Madison walked into Classroom 13. "I don't get it," he said. "What's your costume?"

"Duh," said Mya. "We're a horse."

"One horse?" Mason asked.

"Obviously," said Madison.

Mason scratched his head again. "I know I'm not the smartest kid in Classroom 13. But I don't think horses have *two* heads."

Mya & Madison took one look at each other and started yelling.

"*You* were supposed to be the butt!" Mya shouted.

"No, *you* were supposed to be the butt!" Madison shouted back.

You see, both girls had wanted to be a horse for Halloween. But a horse is a two-person costume. One person wears the head and the front two legs, and the second person wears the back two legs and the butt. But being the butt is hard work. You have to be bent over all day holding the other person's waist. Plus, you can't see anything back there.

Neither Mya nor Madison wanted to be the butt. Instead, both of them wore the *front* half of the costume. So they were a two-headed horse with four front legs and no back legs and no butt.

"You ruined Halloween!" Mya shouted at her twin.

"You ruined our costume!" Madison shouted back.

When the twins began screaming, Ms. Linda peeked out from under her desk. "Oh my!" she said. "Those girls remind me of the terrible wolf that lives in the forest. How frightful! I think I'll stay under my desk until they've gone away."

"Seriously, Ms. Linda?!" Olivia said. "Stop pretending and start acting like a teacher!"

"I don't think she's pretending," said Preeya. "I think she thinks she *really is* Little Red Riding Hood."

"That's ridiculous!" Olivia snorted. "It's not possible."

"Are you sure?" Mason asked. "Look. Hugo turned into a hot dog."

Hugo had turned into a hot dog. And Liam was about to take a bite. Mason slapped the hot dog out of Liam's hands. "Don't eat Hugo!"

Mason put the hot dog in his pocket for safe-keeping.

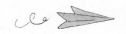

Olivia rubbed her temples. "How did this happen?"

"Who knows?" Dev said, eating some of Classroom 13's candy. He offered the bowl to the fighting twins. "Hey, ladies. Maybe stop screaming and suck on some sweets?"

The twins devoured several pieces of taffy. They stood back-to-back, chewed their taffy, and refused to speak to each other.

What the twins didn't notice was that their costume began to change. So did their bodies. Their skin became soft and covered in light brown hair. Then their arms vanished and their legs grew long. Their feet turned into hooves. Their necks stretched and they stopped chewing. Instead, they neighed.

When Mya & Madison finally looked at each other, they discovered they were connected at the waist and had become a two-headed horse. Frightened, they both tried to run away. Since they were attached, they didn't get far. In fact, they didn't get anywhere.

The whole class was there to witness the transformation. "Holy guac-a-moly!" said Triple J.

"Someone get those girls to a *horse*-pital," Liam joked. "No, seriously, are the twins sick? Maybe they need some cough *stirrup*. Someone get them some medicine. Hurry now, before they fall down and can't *giddyup*!"

"Enough, Liam! This is serious," Isabella said. "Horses shouldn't be cramped inside a tiny classroom. They need to be outside with fresh air and grass and a wide-open space to run around in."

"I'm sorry," Liam said. "I'll stop *horsing* around." Liam cracked himself up. He couldn't stop laughing.

While the other students tried to figure out what was going on, the twins forgot entirely that they had once been human girls. Happy with

being a horse, they walked sideways to the class plants and began chewing the green leaves. If they were really lucky, someone might even give them a carrot or comb their hair.

CHAPTER 5
The (Stinky) Baby

Liam loved laughing. That's why he liked farting so much. He thought farts were hilarious. Sometimes they were loud, sometimes they were quiet, and sometimes they were silent but deadly. No matter how the farts came out, Liam always laughed.

Liam also liked to make other people laugh. Which is exactly why he dressed up as a baby for

Halloween. He came to school wearing nothing but a bonnet, a pacifier, and a diaper. As soon as he walked in, the other students laughed.

"Liam, you crack me up," said Ava.

"Seriously, that is an awesome costume," Teo added.

Jacob didn't laugh. He said, "I don't think babies are funny. I think they're creepy-looking, like little hairless old people."

That made Liam laugh, so he wrote it down. Liam was a joke collector. He had dozens of joke books and had watched hundreds of comedy specials on TV, but his new favorite was improv— where you make jokes up on the spot. Sometimes these jokes came at other people's expense. Today, the butt of his jokes was Mya & Madison, who didn't have a butt anymore. They had some-how become a two-headed horse.

In the midst of another horse joke about Mya & Madison ("Look! The twins are eating with their mouths open. What bad *stable* manners! Bwahahahahahaha!"), Liam began to shrink. A few seconds later, he wasn't just dressed up as a baby—he *was* an actual baby.

"OMG," Emma said. "Liam turned into a baby!"

"Babies are so cute!" said Chloe.

"Look at him!" said Lily. "I just want to eat those fat little cheeks!"

"Do you smell that?" asked Benji. "Oh no! I think baby Liam made a boom-boom in his diaper. I'm not changing him!"

"One-two-three NOT IT!" shouted Santiago.

"NOT IT!" everyone in the 13th Classroom shouted.

"Then who's going to change Liam?" Ximena asked.

No one moved. No one wanted to touch a dirty diaper.

When Liam realized what was going on, he

did *not* laugh. He did not think it was funny at all. Instead, he started crying. And in case you didn't know—a crying baby with a dirty diaper is never, *never* funny.

CHAPTER 6
The Cowboy

Chloe had always wanted to be a cow*boy* for Halloween. But every year her parents bought her a cow*girl* outfit. Chloe thought cow*girl* outfits were lame. They were pink and frilly and had skirts instead of chaps. She wanted a real cow*boy* outfit, with a pair of six-shooters and a mean mustache.

Chloe thought mustaches were cool—which they are.

This year, Chloe ordered her costume herself. She got it online. (Did you know you can get all sorts of stuff online? Like video games and comic books and big tubs of popcorn? You *did* know? Why didn't you tell me?! So rude! Anyway...)

"Cool mustache!" said Lily.

"Cool six-shooters!" said William.

"Are those spurs on the back of your cowboy boots?" Jacob asked. "Awesome!"

"Why, thank ya kindly, pard'ners," she said in a gruff voice.

"What happened to your voice?" Sophia asked.

"Nuttin', honey," Chloe said. "This is how ah always talk."

"Uh, no, it's not," said Emma.

"Uh-oh, it's happened to her, too," Olivia said. "She really thinks she's a cowboy."

"What d'ya mean *thinks*?! Ah *am* a cowboy. Done earned that title after workin' the horse ranch over in Abilene," Chloe growled.

"No, you're not," Olivia said. She pulled at Chloe's mustache. Yet no matter how hard she pulled, it wouldn't come off.

"OW!" Chloe roared. "You're darn lucky you're a lady and ah'm a gentleman and a cowboy. Otherwise, ah'd show ya a thing or two with my fists."

"The mustache is real!" Olivia gasped.

"Yeah, right," Jacob said. "You're just not pulling hard enough." Jacob grabbed Chloe's mustache and gave the hardest yank he could muster. He practically pulled Chloe's face off.

"Mister, ah suggest you run," Chloe growled. She took the lasso from her belt and started swinging it in the air. Jacob barely made it halfway across the room when the rope caught him around the waist. Chloe pulled him in, pushed him to the ground, and tied his hands and feet behind his back and put a sock in his mouth. "Consider yourself hog-tied, mister. And let this be a lesson to ya—never go around pulling a man's mustache. It's darn tootin' rude."

"Am I dreaming?" Mason asked. "This feels like a dream. Like the time I dreamt I came to school naked."

"That wasn't a dream," said Mark. "You forgot to get dressed yesterday."

"Stop talking! Let me think for a minute," Olivia shouted. She rubbed her brain. After all, she was the smartest student in the class. It was up to her to fix things. "Okay. I think people are actually *becoming* their Halloween costumes. But *how*? If we can figure that out, maybe we can reverse the effects."

"What's that smell?" Ethan asked, pinching his nose.

"Ugh. Someone really needs to change Liam," Fatima yelped.

"Ain't no thang," Cowboy Chloe said. "Ah'll take care of it. Can't be worse than helping a mare give birth to a foal."

But Chloe was wrong. As soon as she opened Liam's diaper, a terrible smell overtook the classroom. The smell was so awful that Sophia threw up, which made Ethan throw up, which made Ximena throw up, which made Dev throw up. Surprisingly, Santiago (who was usually sick) did *not* throw up.

"Dang, this is a mess!" Chloe said. "Lucky for y'all, a good cowboy always brings gloves to work...." Chloe put on her gloves and changed Liam's diaper. She opened the door to Classroom 13 and tossed it down the school hallway.

Afterward, everyone cheered. She deserved it. Changing dirty diapers is terrible business. Have *you* ever changed a dirty diaper? I highly recommend skipping it—if you can.

CHAPTER 7
The Mime

What's going on in Classroom 13, you ask? Haven't you figured it out yet?

Yuna did. She wanted to tell the others, but she couldn't. Unfortunately, she had dressed as a mime for Halloween. And everyone knows mimes can't speak.

Of course, Yuna rarely talks anyway. But she *did* know how to communicate in code. So she

scribbled onto a piece of paper and handed it to
Olivia. It said this:

O-DAY OT-NAY EAT-WAY E-THAY ANDY-CAY! IT-WAY
IS-WAY URSED-CAY! E-THAY ANDY-CAY IS-WAY
ANSFORMING-TRAY EOPLE-PAY INTO-WAY EIR-THAY
OSTUMES-CAY! I-WAY ET-BAY E-THAY IRTEENTH-
THAY ASSROOM-CLAY ID-DAY IS-THAY. OU-YAY O-DAY
OW-KNAY IT-WAY ANTS-WAY EVENGE-RAY ON-WAY
ALL-WAY OF-WAY US-WAY, IGHT-RAY?

Olivia took one look at the scrap of paper and
said, "This is gibberish." Then she threw it away.

CHAPTER 8
The Pirate

Being Jayden Jason James—aka Triple J, the most popular kid in school—wasn't easy. Everyone looked to him as a leader. If Dev ran out of lunch money, Dev knew Triple J would loan him a few bucks. If Emma needed a shoulder to cry on? Triple J had her back. Study partner, teammate, gaming buddy. He was all those things because he was dependable. He was the closest thing Classroom 13 had to a class president. He was the best. Well, usually he was...

...but not today.

Today, he was a pirate.

This morning, Triple J strapped on his best hook and eye patch. He made a peg leg out of cardboard and bought a stuffed parrot from the costume store. He painted over some of his teeth and drew a fake beard around his mouth. This was no longer the face of Triple J, beloved hero of Classroom 13. No, no, no. This was now the dastardly mug of Captain Triple J, the Dread Pirate.

When he got to class, his "*Arrrghhhs*" and "*Yo-ho-hos*" were just bad impressions. But soon after coming to Classroom 13, he'd become the real deal.

Olivia didn't know this when she asked him for help. "Triple J, what are we gonna do?"

"*We? Arrrghhhh* ye askin' me to join my crew,

lass?" The Dread Pirate Captain Triple J scowled, poking her ribs with his hook.

"No! I need your help to figure out how to turn everyone back to normal!"

"You can hire me and my mates, all for just five gold doubloons, me hearty," the pirate growled.

"Oh no, not you, too!" Olivia said.

"Fine. Two and a half gold shillings, but that be me final offer, ya scallywag!"

"Jayden, I don't have any gold!"

"NO gold?" he asked her.

"Yes, that's what I've been trying to tell you," she sighed. "I need your help. I don't have time to play pirates."

The dread pirate was deeply offended. He didn't *play* pirate. He *was* a pirate. So he did what any ~~good~~ dread pirate would do: He tied her up, stood her on Ms. Linda's desk, and said, "Time to walk the plank!"

"It's not a plank—it's the teacher's desk," Olivia corrected.

"Enjoy feedin' the fishes, landlubber!" Triple J poked his sword at her back and made her step off the desk.

Olivia rolled her eyes as she landed on her feet and untied herself. She didn't realize how fortunate she was. Dev had planned on dressing up like a *shark*, but the costume got lost in the mail. If it had arrived in time? Well...let's just say things would have gotten messy. *Whew.*

CHAPTER 9
The Tree

Every Halloween, Sophia dressed up as something to remind people to take better care of the planet. She thought it was important to spread a *green* message instead of just saying "trick-or-treat." This year, Sophia dressed up as a tree.

"Why are you dressed as broccoli?" Jacob asked.

"I'm not. I'm a tree," Sophia explained. "I wanted to remind people about deforestation."

"De-for-a-*what?*" Jacob asked her.

"*Deforestation*," Sophia corrected him. "It's when greedy companies destroy forests for selfish gain. This leaves all the little woodland creatures homeless!"

Thinking about those squirrels and chipmunks and raccoons having no place to live made Sophia sad. So she had some candy. As she chewed, Sophia's feet and toes stretched out, digging roots into the classroom's floor. Her hands and fingers rose upward, sprouting into branches. Her hair turned green and grew into leaves.

Sophia had become a real tree, right in the center of Classroom 13.

I'm a tree! she thought. *I'm so happy to be giving all my friends fresh, clean air and plenty of shade. This is wonderf—*

A *tap-tap-tap-tap* interrupted Sophia's thoughts. There was a loud *squeak-squeak-squeak* coming from inside of her stomach.

She quickly realized what had happened. A family of woodpeckers and squirrels was living inside her. She thought, *This is even more wonderful! Now I am a home to animals!*

But as the squirrels ran across her branches, they tore off her acorns with their teensy little claws. *OW!* she wanted to scream. *That hurts!*

The *tap-tap-tap-tap* of the woodpeckers didn't feel good, either. It was like someone knocking on her head with a sharp beak. Nonstop.

It's okay, she thought. *I have become a beautiful, wonderful tree, a home to animals, and what's a little pain if not—YOWZA!! STOP THAT!*

Now a family of caterpillars was eating her leaves. It felt like someone eating her fingernails. Unfortunately, no matter how much it hurt, she couldn't say a word. Trees don't speak. At least not in any language that people or animals understand.

"Excuse me," said Little Linda Riding Hood, "by any chance are you a talking magical tree that can point me toward Grandmama's cottage?"

Sophia couldn't move or say a thing.

Little Linda Riding Hood frowned. "Oh, well. Though you do have a nice trunk. If I find the woodsman, perhaps I can have him chop you down and make you into a nice bench for sitting."

Sophia gulped. She'd always loved trees, but she'd always assumed they had wonderful lives. Now she knew exactly how trees felt—and it was terrible. There was nothing she could do except let the animals eat her.

CHAPTER 10
The Ghost

Video games were Dev's life. He devoted every minute that he could to them. He often forgot important things like brushing his teeth, eating three meals a day, bathing, and, yes, sometimes even flushing the toilet. Gross, right? This is why he forgot to buy a Halloween costume.

You might ask yourself how a kid forgets about the best holiday ever. What could be more important than watching scary movies, or dressing up like a monster, or getting loads of candy for free?

Apparently, Dev's favorite video game franchise's newest release, *Teddy Bear Bashers 3: Zom-Bears*, that's how. It was about an army of brain-hungry teddy bear zombies, and Dev couldn't stop playing.

Luckily, his mom didn't forget, though. She ordered him a shark costume online. Unluckily (for Dev), it got lost in the mail. (Lucky for Olivia, though.)

Dev shrugged. He didn't care that much about Halloween. Until he remembered all the candy and fun he'd miss out on. He shouted, "I need a costume!"

Dev had to get creative. He grabbed a pair of scissors, stole his sister's white sheets, and cut two holes out of them. He threw on the sheet. "That was easy," he said. "Now I'm a ghost."

But he wasn't in class long before he realized he couldn't pick up anything. In fact, he could see right through his own body. "What is happening?!"

Mason accidentally walked through Dev.

Ghost Dev yelled, "Mason! Don't do that! It feels weird."

"Whoa, what happened to you?"

"I...I think I've turned into my costume!" Dev shrieked.

"I think being a cloud is cool," Mason said.

Dev shook his head. "I'm not a cloud; I'm a *ghost*."

Mason screamed and ran away.

Dev rolled his ghost eyes—then realized he could see through the top of his ghost head. He tried to get his classmates to help, but they were all too busy dealing with their own troubles. He tried to get Ms. Linda to help, but she was still looking for the way to her grandmama's house.

Things in Classroom 13 usually sorted themselves out. He just needed to wait. So Dev decided he'd pass the time by playing some video games. He floated to his desk and reached for his portable gaming device. His hand passed through his backpack like air.

"No, this can't be happening!" Dev cried. "What kind of a life is a life without video games?"

"The afterlife?" Olivia asked.

"*AAAAHHHHHH!!!!*" Ghost Dev screamed. "My life is over!"

"Well, yeah," Olivia said. "You're a ghost."

CHAPTER 11

The Princess and the Prince

<del>Once upon a time...</del> Sorry, that's *not* how this story goes. Let me start again...*Ahem*...

"Are you my servant?" Preeya asked Mark. She was wearing a beautiful gown and a tiara on her head. She wasn't just dressed as a princess, she *was* a princess.

"*Excuuuuse* me?" Mark said. He was wearing a velvet cape and a crown on his head. He wasn't just dressed as a prince, he *was* a prince. "Do I *look* like a servant? I'm a prince!"

"You are?!" Preeya said. "Let's get married, then!"

"*Ew.* I don't think so," Mark scoffed.

"What do you mean, '*Ew*'? I'm a beautiful princess, the most fair in all the lands."

"Hardly. And I think you mean *fairest*," Mark corrected her. He looked around the classroom. "Excuse me, strange children. Are any of you my servants? Has anyone seen my knights' guard? Or my castle? I have a royal ball to attend."

"As do I," Preeya said. "I have *lots* of royal balls to attend."

"Not as many as I do," Mark said.

"Even more!" Preeya huffed. "All the balls are *mine!*"

"No, I love balls! The royal balls all belong to *me!*" Mark said.

"Okay, both of you, calm down," Olivia said.

"The classroom is already crazy enough without you two being *royal* pains in my butt. If you don't want to help, then hush."

"*Don't* tell me what to do!" Preeya snapped.

"Are *you* my servant?" Mark said. "I've been standing here for almost five minutes. Standing is hard. My feet are very sore. Will you rub my feet?"

"I will *not* rub your feet," Olivia said. "And I am *not* your servant!"

"No need to be rude," Mark said. "I was only asking."

"*Your* servants are very rude," Preeya said.

"They're not *my* servants," Mark said. "They must be *yours*."

"I think not," Preeya said. "I would never have such *un*attractive peasants work for me. So they must be *yours*."

"I don't think so," Mark said. "You can have them. I'll take the balls."

"You are the rudest prince I've ever met," Preeya said. "I've decided *not* to marry you."

"You can't reject me! I already rejected *you*!" Mark yelled.

"Rejected *me?*" Preeya said. "I'll have my father—the *king*—take off your head!"

"He wouldn't dare!" Mark said. "My mother—the *queen*—would make war with your country!"

"I would rather destroy my country than let you talk to me like that!" Preeya yelled.

"They've gone crazy," Olivia said.

Mason was sitting on his desk with a tub of popcorn. He was eating it slowly with a big smile on his face. "Are you kidding? This is better than reality TV!"

"Who are you, strange man?" Mark asked Mason. "Are you my butler?"

"Your butt-what?" Mason asked.

"My butler. The man who dresses me and calls for my tea and tucks me in at night and reads me stories before bed and—"

"That sounds like a *dad*. I'm not your dad," Mason said.

"Aww, then you must be *my* butler," Preeya said. "Fantastic. Would you fetch me a crumpet and my dog and perhaps a parasol? I think I would like a walk outside, and then—"

"*Whoa*, lady," Mason said. "I'm *not* your butt-thing, either. In fact, no one here works for either one of you."

"Ridiculous!" Mark shouted.

"Incredulous!" Preeya agreed.

"We should have your head removed!" Mark demanded.

Mason shrugged. "Do what you like."

"We should do it," Preeya said. "Let's cut off his head."

"Yes, let's," Mark agreed. "But how? Usually my servants know how to do such things. I don't know how to do such things. Do you?"

"Of course not," Preeya said. "I'm a princess. I don't do the head chopping. That's what servants are for."

"I suppose we could do it ourselves," Mark said. "I have certainly seen several beheadings. But where does one start?"

"I believe we need an ax," Preeya said.

"And then what?"

"I suppose one would have to lift the ax."

"Sounds like a dreadful amount of work," Mark said. "And a lot of it. Who has the kind of strength for something like that? Pick up an ax? What do I look like—a servant?"

"Can you imagine—a prince and a princess— doing *actual* work?" Preeya asked.

Preeya and Mark began to laugh. They laughed and they laughed and they laughed. All tuckered out, the prince and princess fell asleep.

~~And they lived happily ever after.~~

CHAPTER 12
The (Sick) Vampire

When Santiago woke up this morning, he couldn't stop sneezing. He had a fever and a runny nose. His mom said, "You have a cold. Stay home, and I'll make you your favorite: chicken noodle soup."

"No!" he said. "It's Halloween. I don't want to miss the fun." So he ignored his mom and went to school. He didn't realize until lunchtime that he'd forgotten his lunch money.

Silly Santiago. He was always sick. Which is why he usually looked pale. But today, he was more pale than usual. You might even say he looked downright *dead*. That's because he was. Well, close...he was *un*dead. Santiago was a vampire.

At lunchtime, Santiago moaned, "I'm so hungry."

"Ah thought vampires drank blood?" Chloe the Cowboy asked.

"They do," Santiago said. "But, c'mon, *gross*! I want regular food. I want tacos or spaghetti or—what's that in your lunch box? Fried chicken? Yum!"

"Ah'm not sharing muh fried chicken with no fanger, and that there's final!" the cowboy snapped, her spurs jangling as she walked away.

"Can I have a bite?" he asked his classmates.

"No! Get away, Count Sick-ula!" they shouted, grabbing their necks to protect them.

"No, no, no," Santiago tried to explain. "I

meant a bite of your lunch, not a bite of your neck. I swear!"

But it was no use. No one believed him. They heard the word "bite" and they ran screaming. (People tend to do that when they're around vampires.)

Santiago felt a sneeze coming on.... *AAaaaachOOOOOO!!!!*

Except Santiago wasn't a boy anymore. He was a little fuzzy vampire bat. He was flapping his wings. Until...*AAaaaachOOOOOO!!!!*

He turned back into a boy. He fell out of the air and crashed onto the lunch table. "Ow!" he said.

"Get away! I don't want your vampire or your cold germs!" the students shouted, shooing him back.

AAaaaachOOOOOOO!!!! Santiago sneezed again. He turned back into a bat. The kids were throwing pencils and pens at him. He flew up toward the ceiling.

AAaaaachOOOOOO!!!! Santiago sneezed again. This time, he fell from the ceiling all the way to the floor. "DOUBLE OW!" he shouted. Luckily, vampires healed fast. Except apparently from colds.

Emma pulled several cloves of garlic out of her backpack and threw them at Santiago. He was going to eat them, but they weren't cooked. But the smell reminded him of his mom's chicken noodle soup. She was right. He should have stayed home.

CHAPTER 14
The Robot

"Ladies and gentlemen, I now present—L.I.L.Y. Bot!" Lily announced as she walked into Classroom 13. She'd spent weeks making her costume. Using boxes and foil and LED lights and magnets, she'd made herself a robot costume. Using an app on her smartphone, Lily could change her voice. She had different lights and flashlights in the arms. She even had roller skates on so it looked like she was hovering above the floor. She'd thought of everything.

"Best. Costume. Ever!" Fatima said. Everyone agreed.

Of course, like the other students, Lily ate some of the candy when she got to class. She placed the candy in her mouth slot and said, "*Beep-boop*. L.I.L.Y. Bot declares confectionary sustenance is electronically pleasant." This was just fancy robot-speak for "This candy is delicious."

But as soon as the cherry-flavored gumdrops touched her tongue, Lily began to transform into a real robot. Her brain changed into microchips and her skin turned into solid steel. Instead of thinking in human language, she began to think in 1's and 0's.

"*010101011101010101010100101010011*," she said to Olivia.

"Oh no, not you, too," Olivia said.

"*Translating from binary code into language: English,*" the robot said. "*L.I.L.Y. Bot has become real. She is no longer a human child but a powerful robot. This unit feels—magnificent!*"

"Good for you," Olivia sighed. Things were getting worse by the ~~chapter~~ minute.

"Cool! A robot!" Mason said.

"Not cool," Olivia said. "We need to stop what's happening to our classmates!"

"Maybe Mr.—uh, I mean—Miss Robot can help," Mason said. "L.I.L.Y. Bot, you're super smart now. Can you help us?"

"*Negative. This unit has always wanted to go to outer space. Now that I am no longer a fragile fleshy thing, I can. L.I.L.Y. Bot will begin computations to launch through planetary atmosphere and travel to the moon.*" Then she started writing out long mathematical equations on the chalkboard.

"Awesome," Olivia said sarcastically. "We're going to have to figure this out on our own. Thanks for nothing, Lily."

"*You are welcome*," said the robot, continuing her space-travel math.

Later, Little Linda Riding Hood tapped L.I.L.Y. Bot on the shoulder. "Excuse me, Ms. Tin Man? I've heard a story of your helping lost little girls find their way through the woods. Would you help me?"

"*Does not compute*," said L.I.L.Y. Bot.

Little Linda Riding Hood knocked on the robot's metal plating. "You are the Tin Man, aren't you? I'm lost in the woods and I need your help finding Grandmama's house."

"*Are you referring to movie designation:* Wizard of Oz?" L.I.L.Y. Bot asked.

Little Linda Riding Hood knocked on L.I.L.Y. Bot's head. "Sounds like tin to me," she said.

"*Incorrect! Be gone, fleshy thing. I have equations to solve if—beep boop boo—error!*" L.I.L.Y. Bot froze.

"Ms. Tin Man?" Riding Hood asked.

But the robot's lights dimmed. Her limbs fell

to her sides. She could not move. L.I.L.Y. Bot realized that her batteries had died. When Lily had made her costume, she had thought of everything—except the possibility of becoming a real robot and needing a cord to plug in.

CHAPTER 15

The Werewolf

Olivia and Mason didn't know what to do as their classmates continued to turn into their costumes. "What can be causing this?" Olivia asked.

Mason shrugged. "Witches?"

"Hey, don't look at me!" said Ava (who was dressed up as a witch).

"Spelling tests?" Mason asked.

Olivia rolled her eyes. "How does that make any sense?"

"Well, witches use spells, and spelling tests use spelling, so I figured..."

Olivia shook her head. "You really *aren't* the brightest kid, are you?"

Mason shook his head. "Nope. Very much the opposite."

In the midst of their conversation, Olivia and Mason didn't notice that another of their classmates was undergoing a tragic transformation. Benji was transforming from a boy dressed as a werewolf into an *actual*, real-life werewolf.

His clothes ripped and tore to make room for his new wolf muscles. Then he howled at the full moon outside (even though it was daytime). Then he stopped and scratched for fleas.

He sniffed the air. He was hungry. He needed to eat ~~something~~ someone.

He looked around the classroom. There was a pirate and a baby and a two-headed horse. But

Benji wasn't sure what werewolves ate. The pirate looked a little too salty, the baby smelled too stinky, and the horse looked a little too...well, weird. No, none of those would do.

That's when Benji saw Little Linda Riding Hood. She looked delicious.

Benji crept over on his paws, closer and closer. Right as he was about to pounce, Riding Hood saw him. "Well, hello there. By any chance do *you* know the way to Grandmama's house?"

"Who, me?" the werewolf asked. "Uh, yeah, sure. I think it's, uh, well, if you take a right at the hamster cage, and a left at the water fountain, then another left at the chalkboard, and then another right at the pencil sharpener, you should be there."

"Thanks!" Little Linda Riding Hood said. Then she skipped away.

Benji took a shortcut to the other side of Classroom 13 first. He needed to hurry and dress up as a grandmother so he could eat Riding

Hood. Then he realized that didn't make a lick of sense. There was no way someone would mistake a wolf for a person. Not unless they were blind.

By the time Little Linda Riding Hood got there, Benji didn't even bother with dressing up like her grandmother. Instead, he grabbed her and growled, "My, my, my, Riding Hood. What big teeth I have!"

"Hey, that's my line!" Little Linda Riding Hood said.

Then she started to run.

Benji the Werewolf chased her all around Classroom 13. Little Linda Riding Hood screamed, and Benji howled. Chloe the Cowboy would have helped, but she was trying to ride the two-headed horse. Mark and Preeya were still arguing over servants, and the Dread Pirate Triple J was hiding from Dev the Ghost. There was a lot going on.

Anyway...Benji pounced and tackled his

teacher. He bit her leg and started chewing.

"Why are you doing this?!" she cried.

"Don't you know? You're wearing red. It drives animals crazy," Benji explained.

"How have I never thought of that before?" Little Linda Riding Hood asked herself out loud. "It seems so obvious. A camouflage hood would have been a much smarter choice. Also, would you stop chewing on my leg? That hurts."

The werewolf said, "No, I'm hungry."

So Little Linda Riding Hood began screaming.

But what Benji forgot is that werewolves are very different from big bad wolves. When they bite someone, they pass on their werewolf abilities.

So a few minutes later, Little Linda Riding Hood began to change, too. She turned into a much bigger werewolf. Then she started chasing Benji around Classroom 13.

"I can't wait to gobble you up and wolf you down!" the teacher said.

"Could we stop? I'm getting a stitch in my side!" Benji cried.

"No," Little-Linda-Riding-Hood-turned-werewolf growled.

So they kept running in circles, just like dogs do.

CHAPTER 16
The Pumpkin

Principal Pumpernickel had been in his office, trying to take a nice Halloween nap. He was almost asleep when screaming and howling startled him and he fell out of his chair. He was *not* pleased. Interrupting a principal's nap—uh, I mean *work*—was very rude.

When he entered the hallway, he was not surprised to find the loud noises were coming from the end of the hall. There were always strange things happening in the 13th Classroom—but today it was simply too much.

"I'll put an end to these shenanigans!" Principal Pumpernickel said, storming out of his office. He furiously marched down the hallway, tightened his pumpkin necktie, and almost slipped on a dirty diaper. This only enraged him more.

He threw open the door to Classroom 13 and shouted, "What is the meaning of...*this*?!"

Principal Pumpernickel couldn't believe his eyes: Two werewolves chasing each other. A tree in the middle of the classroom. A ghost boy pouting on the ceiling. A crying baby being cared for by a cowboy. A two-headed horse pooping in the middle of the class. And a second later, one of the werewolves changing back into Ms. Linda, dressed as Little Red Riding Hood.

The principal stomped over to Ms. Linda and shouted, "I don't know what is going on, but this is unacceptable! I'm sorry, Ms. Linda, but I think I must fire you!"

Everyone (and every*thing*) in Classroom 13 stood still, including Little Linda Riding Hood, who had *no idea* what was happening.

"Hello, sir, can *you* help me get to Grand-mama's?" the teacher asked.

"Ms. Linda. Enough with the joking. This is a very serious matter," the principal demanded.

"I agree. My grandmama is sick, and I need to take her some soup. Only no one here seems to know where she lives and the woods here are very strange—and that young man there, yes, the furry one, he bit me and turned me into a were-wolf. Very rude, I must say."

Benji the Werewolf lifted up his leg and peed in the corner.

This just made Principal Pumpernickel even more angry. "Ms. Linda! Your class is out of con-trol! You are relieved of your position! You must leave at once!"

Olivia grabbed Mason. "This is serious!" she whispered. "If we don't do something fast, Ms. Linda's going to lose her job for real! It's not her fault the classroom has gone crazy."

"It's not the classroom; it's the *candy*," Mason said.

"What do you mean?" Olivia said.

"Haven't you noticed?" Mason explained. "Every time someone eats the candy here, they turn into their costume."

"Mason, you're a genius!" Olivia said.

"I am not! Take that back!" Mason cried, offended.

Olivia shook her head. "Okay, now we know what's happening, but how do we save Ms. Linda?"

"It's cool, I have a plan," Mason said, reaching into his pocket. He pulled out a hot dog. "*Whoops.* Wrong pocket. Hi, Hugo!" Mason reached into his *other* pocket and pulled out a slingshot. He loaded it up with a piece of licorice from the cursed candy bowl. He took aim and fired the candy straight into Principal Pumpernickel's mouth.

Bop! It was a perfect shot. Principal Pumpernickel swallowed the candy. A moment later, he turned into a giant pumpkin.

CHAPTER 13
The 13th Classroom

Ỵou're probably wondering why Chapter 13 comes after Chapter 16 in this book. There are two reasons:

1. because this is Classroom 13's book, and the 13th Classroom will put its chapter wherever it wants to; and
2. because Classroom 13 wants you to know you can *never* trust a table of contents.

They're not even real tables! They're liars—
just like Honest Lee.

Some believe that *revenge is sweet*.

At least the 13th Classroom always thought so—hence, the idea for cursed candy. A Halloween curse should've brought a smile to Classroom 13's face. It should have been laughing at the misery of the students. But Ms. Linda almost got *fired*!

Now the 13th Classroom felt...well, *bad*.

(Of course, it didn't feel bad enough to stop things.)

(Not yet, anyway.)

CHAPTER 17
Mason

Classroom 13 was pure chaos. Everyone had turned into their costumes—except for two people: Mason and Olivia.

Mason asked, "Why haven't you turned into your costume?"

Olivia rolled her eyes. "Because I'm *not* wearing a costume."

"You're not?"

Olivia shook her head. "No. I'm dressed like me. I don't like Halloween, so I didn't dress up."

"Oh. You're one of *those* people." This time Mason rolled his eyes.

"What about you?" Olivia asked. "Did you eat the candy?"

"Nope. That stuff will rot your teeth."

"I guess that explains why you're normal," Olivia said.

Mason scoffed. "I am not normal; I'm a toothbrush!" It's true. Mason was dressed as a toothbrush.

Some might think this was a weird choice of costume. But personally, I think it's quite clever. There's nothing wrong with clean teeth and fresh breath. Mason brushed his teeth twice a day. Each time he says his alphabet backward while he does it. Then he flosses. He also has a tongue scraper. It makes Mason have the freshest breath ever.

Hrmm. Maybe Mason isn't as dumb as everyone thinks.

"I know you're *dressed* as toothbrush, but you're still Mason," Olivia said.

"No, I'm not! I'm a toothbrush!" Mason argued.

"But you haven't *turned* into a toothbrush, I mean."

"You're starting to hurt my feelings," Mason said. "I'm really proud of my costume."

"*Ugh*, never mind," Olivia said. "I'm just glad you're you. We're the only ones unaffected, so it's up to us. We need to figure out how to undo this...this..."

"Unexpected turn of events?" Mason suggested.

"Yup," Olivia said. "Let's start with the basis for all problem solving: *Where?* Here in Classroom 13. *When?* Today, Halloween. *How?*

With cursed candy. *Who?* I guess that's the big question. And *Why?*"

"What about *What?*" Mason asked.

"What?" Olivia asked.

"Exactly!" Mason said.

CHAPTER 18
The Ninja

Has anyone seen Ximena? What's that? She dressed as a ninja? Oh. That might be a problem. Ninjas are very stealthy. She could be hiding anywhere. (Even right behind you.)

CHAPTER 19
The Knight

Let me tell you the tale of a brave knight. There once was a girl named Isabella Inglebel. Her father suggested she be a princess for Halloween, but Isabella said, "I want to be a knight."

"But you're a *girl*! Girls can't be knights!" her father said.

Isabella and her mother yelled at Mr. Inglebel for several days until he begged forgiveness for his mistake. Then he drove Isabella to the store and bought her the most expensive knight costume they had.

On Halloween, she arrived in Classroom 13 wearing a stunning suit of shining armor, complete with a beautiful silver (plastic) sword.

After eating a cursed chocolate peanut butter cup, Isabella believed that she was a real knight. In fact, she didn't realize she was in a classroom at all. She believed she was roaming the country-side of the enchanted 13th Kingdom—a cursed place of monstrous monsters and distressed damsels and kooky kings.

Isabella the Knight knelt before Mason. "My lord, it sounds as if you and your squire are in need of a noble knight to help you in your quest. I offer my service to thee," Isabella said in a British accent, offering Mason her sword.

Mason was confused. "Was that even English?"

"Yes, it's British," Olivia told him.

"Aha! So it's not English!" Mason said.

Olivia slapped her palm to her forehead.

"How may I help you, my king?" Isabella asked.

"King Mason—I like the sound of that!" Mason said. "All right, Knight, you're hired!"

Isabella the Knight stood. "I shall ride into battle for you, my lord. But first, I require a steed."

"What's a steed?" Mason asked.

Olivia explained, "She needs a horse."

"I've got just the one!" Mason said. He walked her over to Mya & Madison. "It has two heads. So maybe it'll be twice as fast. So, uhhh...I guess, I now pronounce you knight and horse! You may ride the horse!"

Isabella climbed onto the double-necked stallion. It did *not* go well. Both heads wanted to run away from the knight. At the same time. In opposite directions.

Since they were connected at the waist, the horse just spun around in the same spot. Over and over and over again. It was like a two-headed horse tornado. Isabella the Knight hung on to the two manes for dear life and tried not to barf in her helmet.

I wish I could tell you she didn't. But she did.

"I am sorry, my king. This dizzy knight has failed you," Isabella said, retching into her helmet again.

"How can a *night* be dizzy," Mason asked, "especially when it's daytime?"

Olivia slapped her palm to her forehead again. She wondered if they would ever figure this out.

*Hey, look—there's Ximena! Could someone tell her to go back to Chapter 18 where she belongs? What's that? She's too fast? Well, of course she's fast. She's a ninja!

CHAPTER 20
The Mouse

Zoey thought mice were cute. So she dressed up as a mouse for Halloween. Now she *is* a mouse.

At least mice are cute, though, right? Cute and little and *safe*.

Oh. I may have spoken too soon....

CHAPTER 21
The Cat

Some believe that *sharing is caring*. But I, this book's wise and brilliant author, believe sometimes sharing is a *very bad idea*. For instance:

This morning, when Zoey came to class dressed as a mouse, she also brought a little costume for Earl, the class hamster. It was a cat outfit. She announced to the class, "Earl's a cat for Halloween! And I'm a mouse! Aren't we adorbz?" Then she shared some of the cursed candy with him.

Now Zoey was running for her life.

"Oh great, we have a rat problem now, too?" Mason said.

"That's not a rat; it's a mouse. And it's not a mouse; it's *Zoey*!" Olivia explained. She started chasing Earl the ~~Hamster~~ Cat, who was chasing Zoey the ~~Human~~ Mouse. "We have to stop him before he—"

It was too late.

The cat ate the mouse.

CHAPTER 22
The Grim Reaper

Everyone was freaking out. The class hamster ate Zoey! I mean, Earl was a cat, and she was a mouse—what was he supposed to do?

"Guys! Guys! Don't worry. I can fix this," Teo told the class. Of course, Teo wasn't Teo today. Today he was wearing a black cloak and carrying a pole with a long curved blade at the end. (It's called a scythe.) Teo was the grim reaper.

Let me explain...

For Halloween, Teo wanted to be something creepy. His mom said no. But his dad said yes. That's how he got his grim reaper costume. Of course, neither of them let him have any candy at the house. So when he got to school, he started chomping on the cursed candy. He ate more cursed candy than anyone else in Classroom 13. So not only did Teo become the grim reaper, he had his powers, too.

But Teo didn't want people to...you know... *croak*. Especially not his classmates. So he used his powers for good. He would *stop* people from croaking.

Teo turned his scythe upside down. Using it like a golf club, he swatted Earl the ~~Hamster~~ Cat right on the butt—and *POP!*—a hairball flew right out of his mouth. Only it wasn't a hairball; it was Zoey the Mouse.

But the mouse wasn't moving.

"Is she...?" Santiago the Vampire asked. "And if she is, could I maybe have her for lunch?"

Everyone shouted, "NO!"

"What are we going to do?" Olivia asked.

"Just hold your horses," Teo said.

Mya & Madison, the two-headed horse, whinnied and snorted. Teo apologized, "My bad! No offense."

"*Rahhhrrrrrrr-pllllbbrrrrrr*," the two-headed horse neighed. (That was *horse-speak* for "None taken.")

Teo the Grim Reaper got down on his skeleton hands and blew gently on Zoey the Mouse. The mouse coughed once, then twice. She woke up. Then she ran up Olivia's leg and into her hands, where it felt safe.

Everyone clapped. "Teo saved the day!"

"Well, not the whole day," he said, "just a mouse. Now, let's get back to partying!" The others cheered. Some screamed. Benji howled.

"Let's carve this pumpkin!" Teo said, pointing at the pumpkin-formerly-known-as-the-principal.

"No!" Olivia shouted. "And no partying! We're in the middle of a major crisis. But we could use your help."

"No way, dude," Teo said. "I've got better things to do!"

"Like what?" Olivia asked.

"Like *this*." Teo pulled back his hood. Beneath was a skull—but not just any skull. It was the most terrifying skull you can imagine. (After all, he was the grim reaper.) When she saw his face, Little Linda Riding Hood fainted of fright.

"I always wanted a scary costume," Teo said. "And now I have it. The scariest one of all...I'm just *dying* to show my big sister....Get it? Dying. Ha!"

CHAPTER 23
The Witch

Ava loved witches. So for Halloween, she dressed up as one. Then Classroom 13's cursed candy turned her into a real witch—only *not* a very good one.

Upon realizing she was a witch, Ava screamed with glee. She pulled out her wand and said, "What should I do first?"

Preeya and Mark were arguing over who was

more royal. *"You're both royal pains in the logs, so why don't you turn into a couple of frogs!"*

The wand zapped them. Only they didn't turn into frogs. They turned into butterflies. The two fluttered around the room for a bit and then turned back into a prince and a princess—except with big colorful wings.

"Okay, well, I'll try again," Ava said. She looked around the room. Teo had always reminded her of her little brother, so she decided to cast a spell on him. *"Teo the Reaper smells like feets, so let him transform into a bag of dog treats!"*

Once again, the spell went wrong and instead turned Teo into a big ice cube. When he eventually melted, he was going to be mad. Ava was worried. "I should probably get out of here before the grim reaper gets me. At least I have a broom."

But when Ava tried to fly, her broom acted like a wild bronco at a bull-riding competition. It bucked and it bucked until it threw her off. It would have been easier to ride a two-headed horse.

"Being a witch is hard!" Ava said.

It's true. Being a witch is hard. Emma (who was an actual witch) could have told her that, but Emma wasn't herself today. She was—well, we'll get to her soon enough....

You see, a person can't just wake up one day and be a magic-using witch. They have to go to school to learn spells and charms and how to ride a broom. They have to take algebra and biology and practice, practice, practice. It takes years! Now that I think about it, a witch school is just like a real school. Only harder. Witches don't even have weekends off.

But Ava wasn't the type to give up. She was a hard worker, and she didn't mind practicing, even if she got things wrong the first few times.

"Abracabadbra, Alec-Azam, and Fitchety-Switch!

If I'm going to have magic, make me a powerful witch!"

The wand spell flew out, zipped around, and struck Ava. Suddenly she was powerful—and green?! "No, no, no!" she said, running to look at herself in the mirror. Her skin had turned green, her ears had become pointy, and her nose had grown long and covered in warts. "Aww, darn it. My life is a fart," she said.

Her wand made her fart.

"Hey! That wasn't even a spell!" she shouted. She broke her wand in half and vowed to never do magic again.

I guess someone should have warned her—be careful what you *witch* for.

CHAPTER 24
The Blob

Ethan caught Ximena!

Well, he didn't catch her, so much as...well, *swallow* her. Usually, Ethan wouldn't consume his classmates, but it seems to be going around today.

You see, Ethan was just catching up with the "slime" craze. You know—where kids make their own slime using glue and water and stuff from around home. Ethan was obsessed now. He was on the Internet every day looking for new ways to make "slime." Well, for Halloween he made a special batch of see-through green slime—and covered himself in it.

But after downing a couple of cursed sugar straws, he turned into a big blob of slime. Unfortunately, slime can be pretty sticky. So when he moved around Classroom 13, everything stuck to him—

What's that? Why are you interrupting the story? *Oh.* You want to know how to make slime yourself? Well, that's easy. Here's the recipe:

- *Take two slices of bread.*
- *Spread peanut butter (crunchy or smooth) on one slice.*
- *Spread your favorite jelly or jam on the other slice.*
- *Put together. Eat and enjoy.*

What's that? Oh. You're right. That's not a recipe for slime. That's how to make a wha-cha-ma-call-it...a tuna fish sandwich. No, wait. That's not right. Um. What can I say? I'm not a very good cook. That's why I'm a writer. Honestly.

Anyway, as I was saying...

Ethan—the big blob of slime—rolled around and stuck to everything. Which is how he found Ximena. Ninjas may be awesome warriors, but in a battle against sticky slime? Well, let's just say, the score reads like this:

NINJA = 0
SLIME = 1

CHAPTER 25
The Zombie

"I want...to eat...your *braaaaaaaaains!*" Fatima moaned.

Unfortunately, she wasn't kidding. For Halloween this year, she decided to be a zombie. She'd wanted to scare all of her classmates. And she was doing just that.

A hot-cinnamon-flavored candy turned Fatima into a ~~living~~ not-so-living, ~~breathing~~ not-so-breathing ZOMBIE.

"*Braaains...*" Fatima groaned.

Everyone—no matter who they were—was terrified of zombies. And with good reasons. Zombies are terrifying. All the students (and animals) of Classroom 13 ran from Fatima.

Mason tried to run away, but he ran in one big circle. So he ended up running into Fatima. Quicker than she looked, the zombie grabbed Mason and started gnawing on his head.

Mason laughed. "That tickles!"

Fatima kept gnawing and sucking, but a second later she stopped. She moaned, "*Nooooo braaains...*"

"I coulda told you that," Mason said.

Luckily, Cowboy Chloe and the Dread Pirate Triple J were brave. They grabbed the zombie, tossed her in the bathroom, and locked the door.

"*Braaains...*" Fatima cried from the other side of the wall.

She pounded on the door so hard her arms fell off. Don't worry. It didn't hurt. Zombies lose body parts all the time. If they walk too fast, they lose a foot. If they crawl through the mud, they lose a hand. I swear, they'd lose their heads if they weren't attached—oh, wait, never mind, they *do* lose their heads. It's kind of hilarious.

Luckily, Fatima still had her head on. Not that she was using it. After hours of bumping into the door, you would think she would've thought to jiggle the knob with her knee or her foot or her mouth. Or chew through the door. But zombies aren't known for their big ideas.

The thoughts that go through their brains are mostly *"Grrrrrr..."* and *"Hnnnn..."* and *"Braaains..."* and *"6 x 6 x 6 = 216."*

Aha! I was just testing you with that last one. Zombies don't know math. At least I don't think they do.

Poor Fatima. She fell to pieces over her costume. Get it? Fell to *pieces*?

CHAPTER 26
The Viking

The only reason William wanted to dress up as a Viking for Halloween was to wear a fake beard. He was too young to grow a real one, but he wasn't going to let that stop him. He saw a beard in the Halloween store last year, in the wig section, and saved up every quarter and dime until he had enough money to buy one.

He wore it around home, just for fun. The

beard was majestic. When he put it on, he felt like a tough guy. He felt invincible. Unstoppable. Like the king of the world.

As Halloween approached, he decided to wear his beard to Classroom 13. But what were good costumes for people with beards? He looked online.

He could be Fidel Castro—but William didn't want to be a revolutionary. He could be a garden gnome or a leprechaun—but they were too short. He could be Obi-Wan Kenobi—but he didn't want to be a Jedi. He could be President Abe Lincoln—but he was too honest. He could be Santa Claus—but that was the wrong holiday.

Finally, he found the perfect getup. He would be a *Viking*.

When he walked into Classroom 13, he wanted to prove he was a fearless warrior—so he ate worms. Well, *gummy* worms. Well, actually, *cursed* gummy worms.

"Beard the Barbarian Viking is here! Fear and tremble!" he cried. "I've sailed the vast ocean to come and pillage and plunder and raid and rob ya blind!"

"Actually, 'pillage' and 'plunder' and 'raid' and 'rob' all mean the same thing," Olivia noted. "Also, we're kind of busy with a lot of other stuff, so we don't have time to be scared of you. But perhaps you could review some vocabulary words while you wait?"

Olivia handed him a vocabulary book and went back to trying to figure out how to fix everything.

CHAPTER 27

The Wha-cha-ma-call-it?

What is Emma dressed as, you ask?

Honestly, I have no idea.

This whole cursed candy crisis would be over by now if Emma had come as herself for Halloween. If you know Emma, then you know she's an *actual* witch in real life with real magical abilities. (But don't tell anyone. It's supposed to be a secret.) I suppose she could've wiggled her nose, or simply snapped her fingers, or made a smelly potion, or done something witchy to fix everything and turn everyone back to normal.

Instead she came dressed up as a...well, a...I don't know how to describe it. She came as... THAT.

What's THAT?

Well, let's see if I can make sense of THAT.

Emma went into her attic and found all kinds of stuff. She wore a hockey jersey and a nurse's hat. She found an eye patch and a clown wig. She found a tentacle for one arm, and a superhero glove over the other. She had a hairy Bigfoot leg and a chicken leg. Then she added roller skates and wings.

So what was she? *I don't know!* She was... THAT!

THAT's what happened when Emma couldn't decide on just *one* costume for Halloween and came dressed as a hockey-playing, crime-fighting,

roller-skating, high-flying, part-time nurse, part-time clown, Sasquatch-chicken-octopus.

THAT's what *THAT* is.

Emma is either a Halloween costume crazy person—or a total genius. Unfortunately, after eating the cursed candy, she became a crazy person, or crazy *thing*, or let's just call her *THAT*, and started trying to devour (that's a fancy word for "eat") her fellow classmates.

CHAPTER 28
Toilet Paper

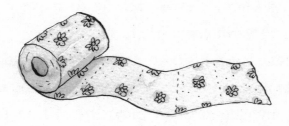

"What should I be for Halloween?" Jacob asked himself that morning while he sat on the toilet. His parents had forgotten to buy him a costume, so he had to make his own. As he went to...you know...*wipe*, he got an idea.

He grabbed all the toilet paper from his bathroom and wrapped himself in it until he looked like an ancient Egyptian mummy.

When he got to school, Fatima said, "Rad outfit."

Triple J said, "Dude, that's awesome. Walk like an Egyptian!"

And Liam, always looking to make a joke, said, "Hey, *Mummy*, where's Daddy?"

Jacob loved his costume. At least he did until he ate an evil lollipop. Instead of turning into a mummy, the cursed candy turned him into a roll of toilet paper.

Luckily, *THAT*—once known as Emma—had no interest in eating toilet paper.

CHAPTER 29
Olivia

As the smartest student in Classroom 13, Olivia knew how to solve most problems.

Algebra? $2 + e + z = $ *Too easy!*

Geography? Olivia knew all the countries and their capitals.

Impossible spelling bee word? How about "succedaneum"? Olivia could spell *s-u-c-c-e-d-a-n-e-u-m* without breaking a *s-w-e-a-t*. Could she use "succedaneum" in a sentence? Yes! "When it comes to spelling, there is no succedaneum for Olivia." (Succedaneum means "substitute.")

But undoing a wicked candy curse on Halloween? Olivia hated to admit defeat, but for the first time in her life, she was stumped. No amount of studying, no amount of library books, no amount of online research could help her find the answer to undo the candy chaos of Classroom 13. But this? This was pure insanity—there was *no* logic here:

Chloe the Cowboy was chasing Benji the Werewolf, who was chasing Earl the Cat, who was chasing Zoey the Mouse. The animals were running everywhere, screaming like...well, *animals*.

Ghost Dev and Teo the Reaper teamed up to scare the pants off the Dread Pirate Captain Triple J. Both ghouls were sorry when they did, though, as his pirate's booty was stinky enough to spook the dead.

The two-headed horse, Mya & Madison, was still horsing around with Isabella the Knight. The horse bucked and twirled, not wanting to be ridden. It trashed the desks and knocked over bookshelves. It finally threw Isabella off the saddle. This was not a *stable* friendship.

Little Linda Riding Hood was holding Little Baby Liam, but he wouldn't stop crying. He needed a bottle and a burping and a nap and a pacifier. "*WAAAAAAAH!!*" he cried. (What a big *baby*.)

William the Viking needed to use the restroom (number two). When he went to the bathroom, he almost let out Fatima the Zombie. He freaked and slammed the door shut just in time. Luckily, he found a roll of toilet paper and was about to go behind Sophia the Tree. Olivia stopped him and said, "Absolutely not! This is a classroom, not a public toilet. And this TP is Jacob!"

Santiago the Vampire was still starving, when he saw a hot dog sitting all alone on a desk. He was about to eat it when Mason slapped him. "Don't eat Hugo!" he shouted.

The prince and princess demanded front-row thrones to all this chaos. Since this was a classroom and not a castle, there were none available. Yuna the Mime silently guided them to sit on top of a Principal Pumpkin and a L.I.L.Y. Bot robot that no one had plugged in.

And then there was the giant slime of Ethan (with Ximena the Ninja still stuck inside) and the Wha-cha-ma-call-Emma (that we call *THAT*)...The three of them somehow managed to get all stuck together. The more they tried to get away, the more they bounced back and got more stuck. Everything they touched got stuck. Books, pencils, desks, backpacks...the whole thing was one giant BLOB. And it was growing by the minute. If Mason (the dumbest student in Classroom 13) and Olivia (the smartest) didn't stop it...it would wreck the whole school!

"Mason, what do we do?!" Olivia shouted. "I can't figure out a way to solve this problem!"

"That's 'cuz you're thinking too hard," Mason said. "It's simple, really. You're the smartest girl in class, which makes you a know-it-all, and since you dressed up like yourself for Halloween, that means you're dressed up like a know-it-all, which means if you eat the cursed candy, you'll become your costume, and you'll be a know-it-all for real, which means you'll know *everything*, which means you'll know how to fix this."

"That...actually makes sense," Olivia said. She grabbed a piece of cursed chocolate and ate it. A second later, she shouted, "Eureka! I am a know-it-all, and I know who did it! The culprit behind all this madness is the Classroom itself.

Its feelings are hurt because it never gets to share in our adventures."

"That's true," Classroom 13 whispered. *"But do you know how to fix things?"*

"I do," Olivia said.

But then the giant blob ate her and Mason. And that was the end of Classroom 13 and all of its students.

The End.

CHAPTER 30
Oh, Wait...

...I forgot there's always a 30th chapter. Plus, I kind of lied. I mean, what would Halloween be without one more trick? The blob didn't eat Mason and Olivia. Not yet, anyway...

The BLOB kept growing and growing until its gooey green head touched the ceiling. It was huge, because anything it touched became part of it. It had swallowed everything and everyone in the 13th Classroom—except Mason and Olivia.

All the kids were inside the giant BLOB and were screaming for Mason and Olivia to do something.

"*But what do we do?*" Olivia shouted back. "I know the who, what, when, why, and where. But I still don't know how to fix it."

Mason said, "Geez. Maybe I'm *not* the dumb one. We hurt Classroom 13's feelings. What do you do when you've hurt someone's feelings?"

Olivia shrugged.

Mason shook his head and turned to the chalkboard of Classroom 13. He said, "I'm sorry."

"*You are?*" the 13th Classroom asked. For the first time, all the students heard the Classroom.

"Of course," Mason said. "Tell me, why'd you do all this?"

After a long pause, the 13th Classroom

explained, *"Because I'm jealous. I want to have fun, too."*

All the students (and Ms. Linda Riding Hood) gasped. Olivia couldn't believe her ears. This... this didn't make any sense! How could a...a... *classroom* have feelings?

"I'm tired of being left out," the 13th Classroom continued. *"Money, wishes, fame, superpowers. What classroom wouldn't want to be part of all that? But every time, you forget about me. You never invite or include me. That's why I wanted my revenge, so I cursed the candy. I wanted to punish all of you."*

"That's it?" Mason said. "Silly Classroom 13. You should have spoken up sooner. If you want to join our adventures, you should!"

"You mean, you'd still want to include me? Even after all this?" Classroom 13 asked.

"Yup," Mason said. "I mean, I thought today was pretty fun. I'm looking forward to whatever happens next. You should, too."

"*But how can I be part of it?*" it asked.

"You have all these magic powers, right? You changed us into our costumes. So why can't you change yourself into one of us?"

The 13th Classroom had never thought of that before.

"But first," Mason said, "you have to change everyone back. Deal?"

"*Deal,*" said Classroom 13.

SWOOOOOOOOOOSH! A magical cyclone formed inside the classroom. Bright smoke and sugary whirlwinds turned and reversed the curse, transforming everyone from costumed *Hallow*-weirdoes to just weirdoes wearing Halloween costumes. (Or in Hugo's case, Hallow-*weiner* costume.)

"Oh, one last thing," Mason asked. "Could you erase the adults' memories of today? We really like Ms. Linda. We don't want Principal Pumpernickel to fire her."

"*Sure thing,*" Classroom 13 said.

Formerly-a-Pumpkin Principal Pumpernickel returned to his office to finish his nap. When he woke, he thought he'd had the strangest dream but couldn't remember any of it. And Ms. Linda didn't recall anything. So even though it was almost the end of the school day, she took roll call. That's when she noticed something was off.

Ms. Linda took a head count of her students. "...Twenty-six, twenty-seven, and *twenty-eight?!*" She counted again. Twenty-eight.

"That can't be right," she said. "I only have *twenty-seven* students."

"Not anymore," Mason said. There was a brand-new face in Classroom 13—a strange young student with a cube instead of a head.

"Who are you?" Ms. Linda asked.

"My name is 13," the student said. "I'm your new student."

To be continued...

And now a special message from author Honest Lee

Did you ever figure out Yuna's code in Chapter 7? Olivia thought it was gibberish, but it wasn't. It was an actual language. (Kinda.) Okay, so maybe it's not a real language but it is a code—and we all know Yuna loves codes.

Here's a hint: **Oink-oink!**

Get it?

You don't?! (You are infuriating. But I still like you.) (Kinda.)
I'll give you another hint: ig-Pay atin-Lay.

Now do you get it?

No. Then never mind. Buh-bye!

Sigh.

FINE!

I'll tell you how to speak in Yuna's code. But only because I think it would be funny if every kid on the planet started speaking in Pig Latin and no adult anywhere knew what was going on— except me.

*So, Yuna's code is **Pig Latin**. Here are two easy steps to learn it.*

1: Words beginning with vowels (a, e, i, o, u):

Simple. Just add "-way" to the end of the word. Here are some examples:

*The word "ick" becomes **ick-way**. The word "egg" becomes **egg-way**. And the word "uncanny" becomes **uncanny-way**.*

*This also holds true for the personal pronoun "I," which becomes **I-way**.*

2: Words beginning with consonants (that's any other letter that is not a vowel):

Simply move the consonant (or consonant cluster) to the end of the word, then add "-ay" to the end of that. Examples:

- Words beginning with consonants would change as follows: The word "hello" would become **ello-hay**. The word "house" would become **ouse-hay**. And the term "Pig Latin" would become **ig-pay atin-lay**.

- Words beginning with consonant clusters would change as follows: the word "school" would become **ool-schay**. The word "transform" would become **ansform-tray**. And the term "fruit smoothie" would become **uit-fray oothie-smay**.

Got it? Good! Now go speak in code and freak out your parents!

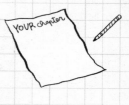

CHAPTER 31
Your Chapter

That's right—it's your turn!

Grab some paper and a writing utensil. (Not a fork, silly. Try a pencil or pen.) Or if you have one of those fancy computer doo-hickeys, use that. Now tell me...

What is YOUR costume for Halloween?!

When you're done, share it with your teacher, your family, and your friends. (Don't forget your pets! Pets like to hear stories, too.) You can even ask your parents to send me your chapter at the address below.

HONEST LEE
LITTLE, BROWN BOOKS FOR YOUNG READERS
1290 AVENUE OF THE AMERICAS
NEW YORK, NY 10104

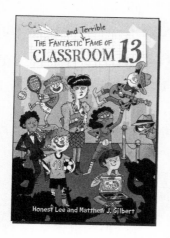

Don't Miss Book 6!

The SWEET AND LOVELY ~~Rude and Ridiculous~~ ROYALS OF CLASSROOM 13

Honest Lee and Matthew J. Gilbert

Available soon!